# Tom Thumb

illustrated by Claudia Venturini

**Child's Play (International) Ltd**
Swindon          Auburn ME          Sydney
© 2007 Child's Play (International) Ltd     Printed in China
ISBN 978-1-84643-196-8 (h/c)   ISBN 978-1-84643-116-6 (s/c)
3 5 7 9 10 8 6 4 2
www.childs-play.com

Once upon a time, a baby boy
was born to a farmer and his wife.
They were very proud of their new child.

He was so tiny that
they called him Tom Thumb.

Tom was very clever and helpful, and very good company.

He used to go and work in the fields with his father.

They would load
wood into the cart.
When it was full,
Tom whispered
in the horse's ear
to guide it home.

One day, some circus people saw
Tom standing in the horse's ear.
"That's amazing!"
they said to each other.
"He could be really
useful in our circus!"

They offered to buy Tom from his father, but he refused. Tom, however, had other ideas.

"Take the money!" he whispered. "It will help to fill the larder. Don't worry. I'll find a way home!"

So Tom's father took the money, and Tom rode off on the circus owner's tall top hat. As soon as they came to the circus, the man put his hat on the ground. Straight away, Tom jumped off and ran away as fast as he could!

Tom hid in a mouse hole.
The whole circus looked for him, but to no avail.

Tom decided to spend the night in a snail's shell.
Before he went to sleep, he overheard two robbers
plotting to break into a house.
Tom thought that he would spoil their plan.
"Hello!" he shouted to them. "I can help you!"

"How can a little thing like you help us?"
sneered the robbers.
"Simple!" said Tom. "Just lift me up to the window,
and I'll throw out whatever you want!"

The robbers put Tom up to the window,
and he crept silently through the bars.

He found himself in the milk maid's
bedroom. She was fast asleep.
He shouted as loudly
as he could, to wake her up.
"What do you want me to steal?"
he called to the robbers.
"Anything special?"

The noise woke up the maid, but she could not see Tom. She looked out of the window, and saw the robbers waiting in the shadows. Picking up a broom, she chased them far into the night.

"At last!" thought Tom. "Time for a rest!"
He found a hay loft, and settled down in some
dry, warm hay. Soon, he fell fast asleep.

He was woken roughly from his slumbers
the next morning. It was time to feed the cow,
and the milk maid picked up the hay,
with Tom inside it. The cow gobbled it all up!

Luckily, the cow's teeth missed Tom, but it was very cramped and dark in her stomach.
He did not despair, but used a bit of hay to tickle her throat, until she coughed him out!

He had no sooner landed in the hay,
than a wolf came along and gobbled him up!
"I'm not sure which is worse," thought Tom.
"The inside of a cow or the inside of a wolf!
But I think I can save myself a long walk."
"Mr Wolf!" he called out.  "Can you hear me?"
"Yes, I can," answered the wolf.
"But who are you?  And where are you?"

"I'm your stomach," pretended Tom.
"Listen to me, and I will take you to a place where
you can eat and eat until I am full."
All night, the wolf ran across hill and dale,
until it was outside Tom's house.
"Here we are!" said Tom.  "Climb in through that vent,
and you will find as much food as you want!"

The wolf ate and ate, until it was morning.
"Time to go!" shouted Tom, "or they'll catch you!"
The wolf tried to wriggle out backwards, but it
had eaten so much food, that it became stuck.
"Spit me out!" called Tom. "Then you can escape."
But still the wolf could not budge!

All the commotion woke Tom's parents.
"It's a miracle!" they shouted. "Our boy is back!
We thought you were lost. Where have you been?"
"Well," said Tom. "I've been in a mouse hole,
a robber band, a hayloft, a cow's stomach
and a wolf's belly! Which reminds me, can you help
my friend to escape?"

They pulled and pulled,
until at last the wolf came free.

"Let's have breakfast," said Tom's parents,
"while you tell us all about it. Did you enjoy
your great adventure?"
"It was exciting," Tom laughed, "but it's very good
to be home!"